CW00457901

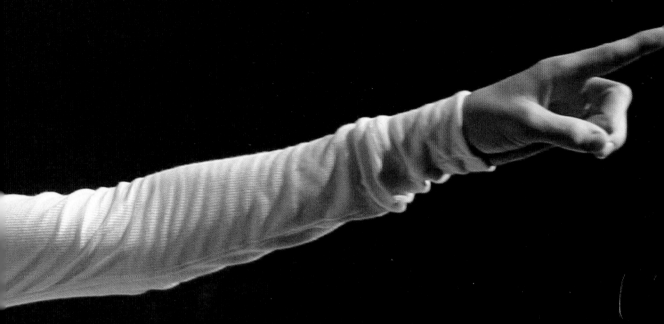

£7.99

A Pillar Box Red Publication

© 2012. Published by Pillar Box Red Publishing Ltd.

ISBN 978-1-907823-29-9

Images © bigpictures.co.uk and Shutterstock.com

Additional images: Vectorportal.com / allvectors.com / Matt Gruber / Creation Swap / Lars Karlsson / Iris Kawling / Robertas Pezas / espensorvik / Steve F / Massimo Finizio / New Brunswick Tourism / MamaGeek

we ♥ you...
JUSTIN BIEBER
A 2013 ANNUAL

WRITTEN BY SARAH DELMEGE
DESIGNED BY GERRY HILLMAN

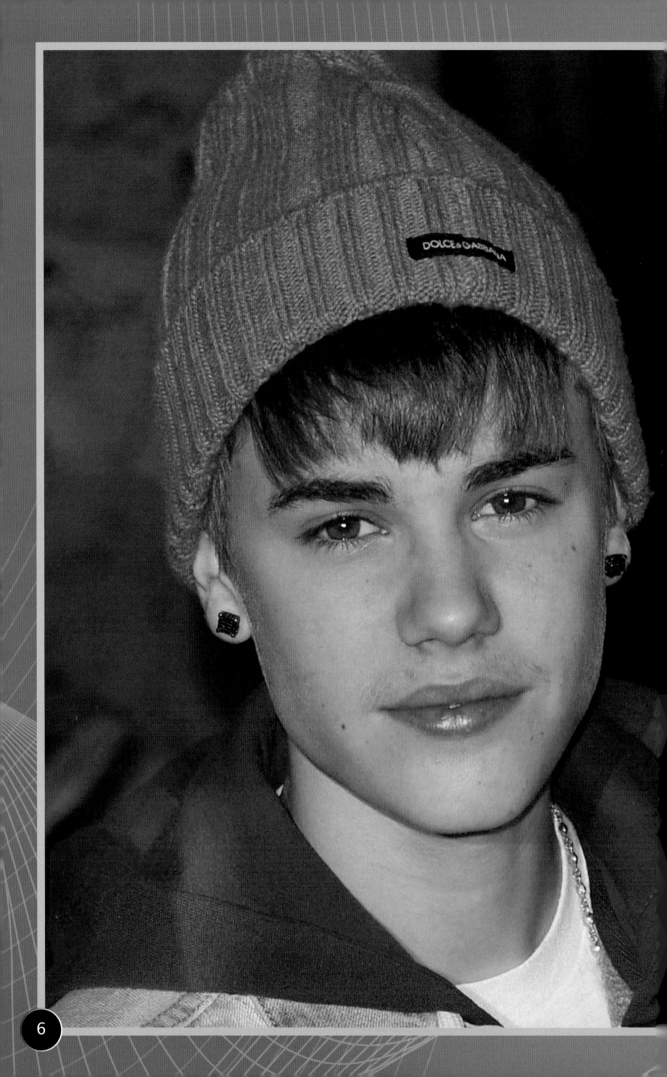

CONTENTS

we love you...

JUSTIN BIEBER

BECAUSE...

You're not afraid to try different things

You have gorgeous hair

You stand up for what's right

You're amazingly talented

You can throw some serious shapes

You want to make the world a better place

You have super dedicated fans

You're stylish

The Bieber Bible:

Full name: **Justin Drew Bieber**

Date of birth: **1 March 1994**

Hair: **Brown**

Eyes: **Brown**

Nationality: **Canadian**

Hometown: **Stratford, Ontario, Canada**

Fave colour: **Purple**

Fave food: **Spaghetti bolognaise, cheesecake**

Fave drink: **Orange juice**

Fave number: **6**

Shoe size: **7.5**

Idol: **Former hockey player Wayne Gretzky**

Pets: **A papillon dog called Sam**

Secret talent: **Can solve a Rubik's Cube in under a minute**

Fave music video: **Michael Jackson's Thriller**

Inspirations: **Grandpa and Usher**

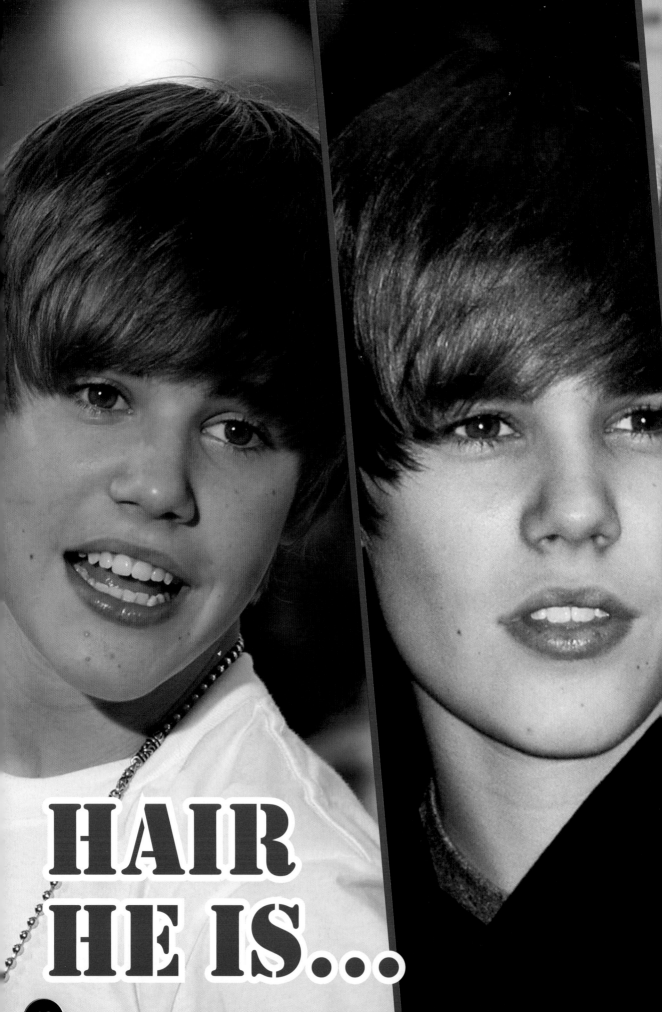

HAIR HE IS...

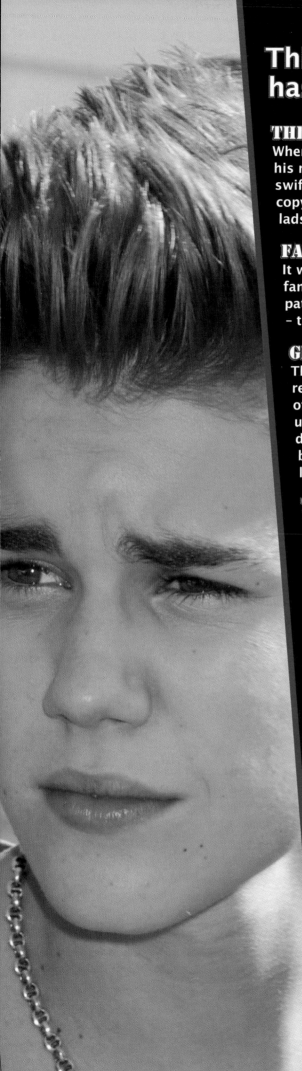

This boy never has a bad hair day...

THE BIEBER

When Justin launched on to the scene, it wasn't just his music which swept the nation. Justin's hairstyle swiftly became the hottest boy look around. Bieber copycats popped up all over the place with some lads paying over £150 for the must-have trend!

FANTASTIC FLIP

It wasn't just Bieb's original hair that caught his fans attention - there was also the hair-flip down pat. Also known as the Twitch, Flip, Switch or Flow - the Bieber hair flick was everywhere.

GETTING THE LOOK

The secrets of Justin's trademarked 'do' were revealed in a promo video for MTV's The Diary of Justin Bieber. In the clip, Justin styles his hair using a combination of towel-drying, blow-drying and mussing. "After I shower," he says "I blow dry my hair and just shake it and it goes like that."

THE CUT

When Bieber trimmed his legendary locks, no one predicted the mass hysteria that trimming off the star's hair caused. Those little pieces of Justin ended up selling for a staggering $40,668 after 98 bids with all the proceeds going to animal rescue organisation, The Gentle Barn Foundation.

HAIR TODAY

Justin is turning into an adult and he wants his style to reflect that. He doesn't want to be defined by his hairstyle. "People are always like, 'So, your hair is your trademark' and stuff. I'm like, 'No. My voice is my trademark, you know?" These days, Justin's hair is sleeker and slightly darker. We like.

DID YOU KNOW?

When JB chopped his side-swept coif, nearly 80,000 fans were so upset they stopped following him on Twitter!

THE CREW

Ever wondered what Justin would look like with a crew cut? Check out some of his old YouTube videos such as "Justin singing Because of You by Ne-Yo" for a hair-raising sight.

13

THE BIG CROSSWORD
Test your JB knowledge with this mega puzzle.

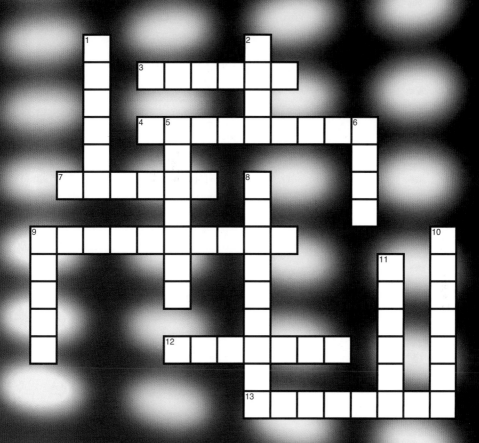

ACROSS

3 Justin's star sign (6)

4 The name of Justin's hometown (9)

7 Mummy Bieber (6)

9 One of Justin's favourite sports (10)

12 The name of Justin's celebrity fragrance (4,3)

13 Bieb's favourite footwear (8)

DOWN

1 Justin's gorgeous girlfriend (6)

2 The Bieb is ____ handed (4)

5 How Justin stays connected (7)

6 Justin's middle name (4)

8 A name for Justin fans (9)

9 Scooter ____. Justin's manager (5)

10 _____ of Promise, Justin's fave charity (7)

11 Justin's favourite colour (6)

Answers on Page 61!

FAMELINE
Justin's rise to fame...

2007: THE YOUTUBE YEARS
Justin's mum uploads a YouTube video of him singing at a local talent show. After getting a positive response, Justin begins putting up more videos of himself singing and playing on YouTube.

2007: MEETING SCOOTER
Later that year, marketing executive Scooter Braun clicked on one of Justin's videos, purely by accident. Scooter contacts Justin's mum.

2008: BIEBER GETS USHERED
Scooter sets up a meeting between Justin and Usher. Impressed, Scooter signs Bieber to Raymond Braun Media Group and then to Island Records. Justin moves to Atlanta.

OCT 2009: TODAY SHOW
Justin makes a career milestone when he performs live on the Today show.

JANUARY 2010: GRAMMYS
Justin makes his first ever Grammy appearance, alongside Ke$ha.

FEBRUARY 2010: OH, BABY
Justin releases the music video for his hit, Baby. It features appearances from Drake, Jasmine V and Ludacris and becomes the most watched YouTube video of all time.

2010: MY WORLD TOUR
Justin launches his first international tour.

APRIL 2010: BIEBERMANIA
Justin causes riots in Australia when he appears in the country.

DECEMBER 2010: YOUNG LOVE
Rumours that Justin is dating Selena Gomez begin surfacing.

JANUARY 2011: GOLDEN GLOBES
Justin makes his first appearance at the Golden Globes, presenting Best Animated Film alongside Hailee Steinfeld.

FEBRUARY 2011: BIG SCREEN STAR
Justin's first biopic, Never Say Never, is released in 3D.

NOVEMBER 2011: UNDER THE MISTLETOE
Bieber releases his first holiday album.

JUNE 2012: NUMBER ONE
Justin's album Believe sold 374,000 copies in its first week – the biggest debut sales week for any album in 2012.

SEPTEMBER 2012: ON TOUR
Justin starts his epic sell-out Believe tour.

HIS WORLD

Meet Justin's trusted inner circle.

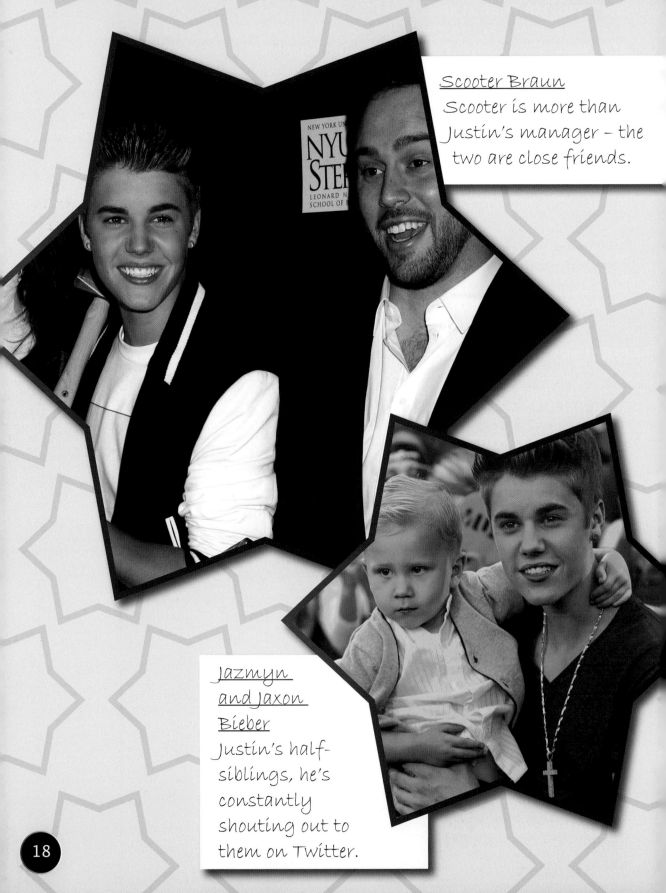

Scooter Braun
Scooter is more than Justin's manager – the two are close friends.

Jazmyn and Jaxon Bieber
Justin's half-siblings, he's constantly shouting out to them on Twitter.

Selena Gomez
Justin's girlfriend knows a thing or two about what it's like to be ultra famous.

Usher
Friend and mentor, Usher has remained a constant source of guidance for Justin.

His mum
No one is more important to him than his mum, Pattie. Justin says she knows how to keep him in check.

WRITTEN IN THE STARS

Read on to see how Justin's success was meant to be!

Pisceans have great compassion, which is no doubt where Justin gets his kind, generous and patient spirit. Pisceans are also extremely imaginative and empathetic, enabling them to understand the difficulties and hardships in other people's lives by putting themselves into other people's shoes. Justin definitely knows he has the ability to relieve the suffering of others which is incredibly important to him and he gets a lot of pleasure through working with and supporting charities.

AS A PISCES, JUSTIN IS:
Shy, romantic, trustworthy, aloof, dreamy, creative, understanding, unrealistic, unpractical

LIKES:
Romance, nature, music, poetry, being loved/wanted, freedom, privacy

DISLIKES:
Dirt, tight spaces, authority, revealing private life to paparazzi

Pisceans are also known for their charming personality and good sense of humour – anyone who knows Justin would agree.
Also, their amazing talents in art, music or crafts often leads to a brilliant career, if they are just prepared to reach out and grasp their moment in the spotlight. We're so glad that Justin reached out for his.

Can you imagine a world without JB?

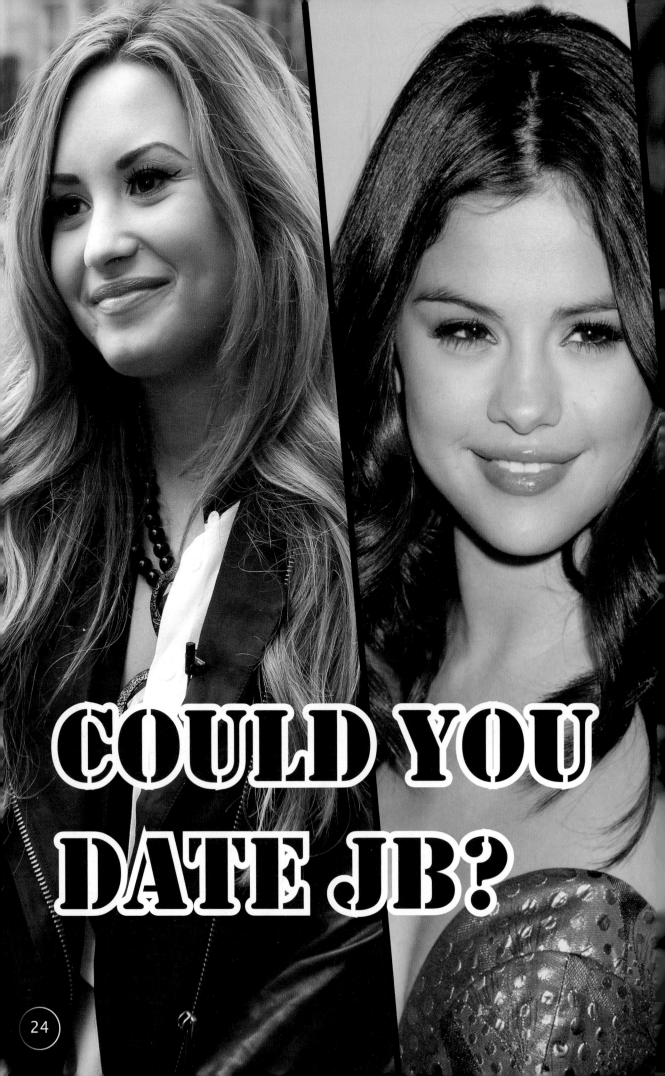

COULD YOU
DATE JB?

24

Find out if you could be JB's date to prom, red carpet event or for a day of fun...

How would you describe your make-up style?
(A) Daring. You're into sparkles, eye shadow and eyeliner.
(B) Classic. A sweep of mascara and some lip gloss is all you need.
(C) Simple. A moisturiser with sunscreen has it covered.

If you could spend a day with a teen movie queen, who would it be?
(A) Miley Cyrus. She knows how to command attention.
(B) Selena Gomez. She'd be an amazing best friend.
(C) Demi Lovato. She loves adventure.

If you had an entire weekend free, how would you spend your time?
(A) Shopping and getting manicures with your girls.
(B) Snuggled up, watching your favourite DVD.
(C) Organising a spur of the moment camping trip.

What is the one thing you wouldn't be seen in?
(A) Anything last season, dah-ling.
(B) Sequins. You hate to stand out.
(C) Skirts. You're way more of a jeans and sneakers girl.

What's your idea of a perfect date?
(A) A romantic picnic.
(B) Getting tickets to the hottest concert in town.
(C) A theme park.

Your friends are most likely to describe you as:
(A) Sweet.
(B) Drama queen.
(C) Adventurous.

Mostly As
Red Carpet
As someone who loves to get noticed, it makes sense that you could accompany the hottest young pop star to major events. Make sure you get to know Justin too though.

Mostly Bs
Prom Date
A girly girl to the core, the perfect date for you and Justin would be a prom. You're a total romantic at heart and you bring out the softest side of everyone around you. Justin would be proud to be your Prom King.

Mostly Cs
Adventure Date
You're an outgoing girl with a taste for adventure. Justin has already shown us how much he loves a challenge. Why not try bungee jumping, riding the roller coasters at the amusement park or some other extreme sport.

25

THE TWEETEST MOMENTS
Justin really does say the Tweetest things!

"#beforeihadmyfans I didn't know living my dream was possible, so thank you."

"Music is the universal language no matter the country we are born in or the color of our skin. Brings us all together."

"I'M SEXY AND I KNOW IT."

"Having a moment. Just grateful 2 b here living this life. Not gonna waste the opportunity. Not gonna be selfish. Not gonna get in my own way."

"No ones on the level that my fans r on."

"I'm not shaving for a month so you can all see my mustache...I'm pumped."

"I think I understand im not living a normal life anymore...but im normal. People say all sorts of stuff but I know who I am and Im grateful."

"swaaaaaaaaaaaaaaaaaa aaaaaaaaaaaaaagggggg ggggggggggggggggggg gggggggggggggggggggg ggggggggggggg!"

"Anyone looking for Prince Charming? Well hello there. Haha. #SWAG."

"Je t'aime BELIEBERS!"

FACT OR FICTION?

Reckon you know your Biebertruths from your Bieberlies?

Check this little lot out...
Find the Answers on Page 61!

(1) Justin released an iPhone app to accompany his Someday fragrance launch.

(2) Justin can count to ten in German.

(3) Justin's last name is actually Biebern.

(4) Justin can speak French.

(5) Justin has performed privately for Prince Harry.

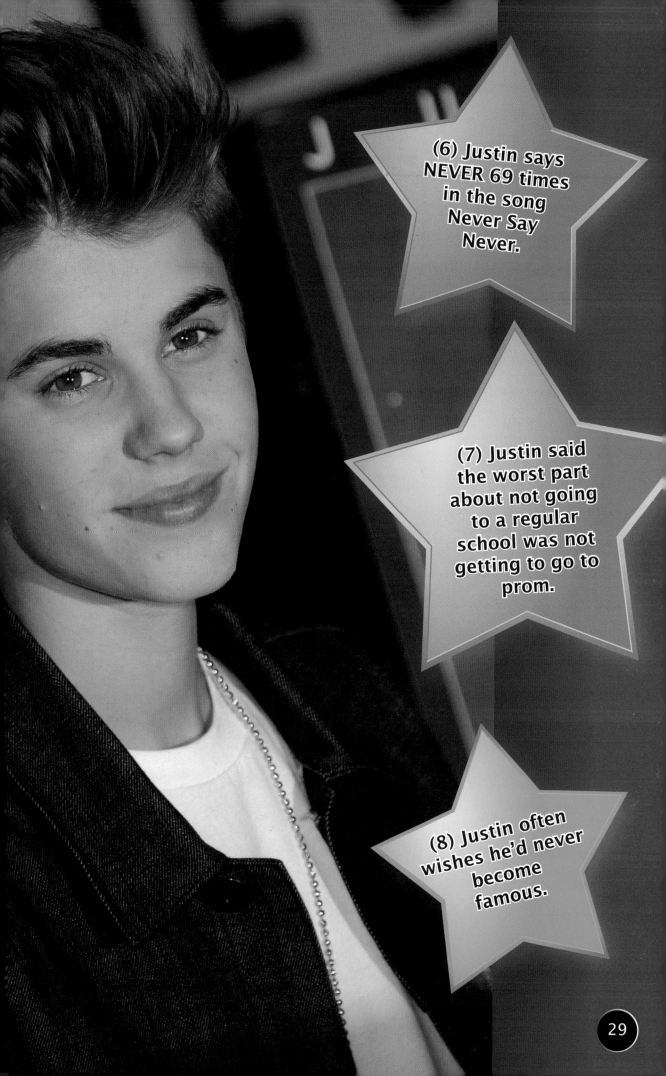

(6) Justin says NEVER 69 times in the song Never Say Never.

(7) Justin said the worst part about not going to a regular school was not getting to go to prom.

(8) Justin often wishes he'd never become famous.

29

SPOT THE DIFFERENCE

See if you can spot the eight differences between these two Biebertastic pics!

Answers on page 61!

HOT HOBBIES

Ever wondered what the Prince of Pop does in his spare time?

ICE HOCKEY

Coming from Canada, it's no surprise that Justin is also a huge ice hockey fan. He's a huge supporter of the Toronto Maple Leafs.

WATCHING TV

When he's got some downtime, Justin likes nothing better than catching up with his favourite TV shows. He always tries to keep up with his favourites, including Grey's Anatomy, American Idol and Smallville.

GO-KARTING

Justin might be old enough to drive these days, but long before he had a license to drive on the road, he raced go-karts with his friends.

BASKETBALL

He's renowned for his ball skills and whenever he gets a spare moment, there's nothing he likes better than shooting some hoops. His favourite team is the LA Lakers and can often be spotted watching his team courtside.

GOLFING

Justin can often be found on the golf course. He loves the sense of peace and relaxation he gets whilst playing this sport.

SKATEBOARDING

When Biebs isn't riding his Segway, you'll often find him speeding down the sidewalk on top of a sleek skateboard.

FASHION PLATE

No doubt about it, this superstar has a serious sense of style!

The Bieb has changed more than just his iconic hairstyle over the last few years. As he and his music continue to grow, the style that Justin rocks continues to get even more fresh and exciting.

The singer has developed an ever-evolving sense of style from fitted caps and plain T-shirts to patterned suits, eye-popping sneakers, geeky glasses and high-top trainers. Whether he's going for the boy next door look or for a sophisticated swag, the singer wears everything with an extra layer of confidence.

Justin's top style tips

NATURAL BORN WRAPPER
Justin doesn't clumsily sling his scarf around his neck. He knots his neckwarmer, threaded through a loop.

THE MULTI-TALENTED JACKET
The Bieb knows how to get the most out of a jacket. He rolls up the sleeves and wears with a pair of coloured jeans.

WELL-FRAMED
One way Bieber adds a little more character to his style is by throwing on some bold substantial frames.

LAYERING
Justin understands the power of a cardigan. Almost any time with anything, it's a fool-proof layer.

ACCESSORIES
He loves pocket chains, watches, dogtags, chains, sunglasses – Justin knows how to transform any outfit with jewellery.

LIVE YOUR LIFE THE JUSTIN WAY

The Biebernator has learnt a lot on his way to superstardom...

TRY NEW THINGS

He may be a global superstar, but Justin is always keen to try new experiences whether or not he's good at them. "You have to let yourself do stuff you're not good at." he says. Although we reckon there's not much that Justin's not good at.

YOUR MUM IS ALWAYS RIGHT

Justin is incredibly close to his mum who has supported him throughout his superstar journey. As Justin says: "My mom is an absolute sweetheart and is always there for me." No wonder Pattie's so proud of her little boy.

KEEP IT REAL

Despite being one of the biggest stars on the planet, he's still utterly normal. "I'm still a regular kid. I don't expect, nor do I want, anyone to treat me differently." Just one of the many reasons why we love you, JB. Sigh.

EMBRACE WHO YOU ARE

He may be a fully–fledged popstar, but Justin still has to put up with people saying nasty things just like the rest of us. He doesn't let other people get him down. "Haters will say what they want, but their hate will never stop you chasing your dream." Hear, hear.

FIND YOUR OWN STYLE

Justin has never been a slave to trends, preferring to wear what he likes instead. "Style can be how you carry yourself," he says, " and how you wear whatever you have on." JB knows the key to looking great is confidence and we couldn't agree more!

HOW TO SPEAK BELIEBER

JB is such a star, he even has his own language.

BIEBERLICIOUS:
Another word for describing something which is hot.
Use it: Justin looks Bieberlicious in his new video.

BIEBERNATOR:
A nickname given to Justin by his Beliebers.
Use it: How can you not be a fan of the Biebernator?

BIEBERTASTIC
A way of describing something which is amazing and totally Biebery.
Use it: My life is so Biebertastic!

OJBD
Term to describe Obsessive Justin Bieber Disorder.
Use it: Molly is suffering from OJBD.

BELIEBER
An obsessive Justin Bieber fan, also see Biebette.
Use it: I am so an absolute Belieber

BIEBER FEVER
The effect Justin has on his fans all over the world.
Use it: Bieber fever is sweeping the nation!

BIEBERFIED

To write Justin's name on your personal possessions or person.

Use it: I totally Bieberfied my bag.

BIEBERSTRUCK

The moment a Bieber fan realises they are in love with Justin.

Use it: I was totally and utterly Bieberstruck.

BIEBETTE

An obsessive Justin Bieber fan, also see Biebetter.

Use it: She's a total Biebette, so obsessed!

EAGER BIEBER

A fan who will do anything to meet Bieber.

Use it: I'm such an eager Bieber – I got to his signing at 3am!

SCRAMBLED LYRICS

WE'VE SCRAMBLED UP SOME SONG LYRICS –
CAN YOU GUESS WHICH SONGS THEY'RE FROM?
ANSWERS ON PAGE 61!

1. DIDN'T BELIEVE WHERE YOU WOULD BE I

2. YOU ME LOVE KNOW I CARE YOU KNOW YOU

3. PLACES BEFORE I YOU CAN NEVER AIN'T TAKE YOU BEEN

4. HOW YOU CHANGE ME TELL MAKE HEY A TO CAN

5. MO EENIE CAUSE LOVA MINEY IS A MEENIE SHORTY

JUST IN LOVE

Make way for the cutest couple in pop. Jealous much?

Justin Bieber and Selena Gomez might have started off as friends, but they are now one of the most adorable couples in young Hollywood.

There's no doubt their relationship is incredibly special. She's taken him to Texas to meet her family and Justin's taken her to Stratford to meet his. They've gone to each other's concerts and he took her to see an NJL hockey game and to an exclusive date at the 20,000 seat Staples Center in LA where they dined and watched Titanic on a massive screen. The couple like to keep their relationship private, but they are obviously crazy about each other. Justin recently opened up abut how deep in love with Selena he REALLY is.

"What does love feel like? It feels good," says Justin. "If you're really in love then you should get butterflies. Butterflies and happiness, that's how I feel anyway. But I never like to throw it in my fan's faces. I love my fans and I'd never want to do that to them. It's my private life and I like to keep it separate. I don't have many things that I get to keep to myself, but that's one thing. I'm very happy and I know my fans just want to be happy for me."

How sweet is that? No doubt about it, Justin is the cutest boyfriend ever. Sigh.

MUSICAL INFLUENCES

These are just some of the musical legends that have made a lasting impression on Justin...

MICHAEL JACKSON
Justin is a superfan of MJ. He loves Michael's powerful voice, superhuman dance moves and the universal appeal of his music.

USHER
Justin has learnt a lot from Usher, who has been a recording artist since his teens, not to mention a dance move or two.

THE BEATLES
The top-selling musical artists of all time, the Beatles pushed the very boundaries of what music could be. Justin is a huge fan.

PRINCE
Another amazingly talented idol, whose performances are legendary. Similarly to Justin, Prince has quite a liking for purple.

BOYZ II MEN
One of the most successful boy bands in the 1990s. They produced a string of smash hits, including Motownphilly, The End of the Road, It's So Hard to Say Goodbye to Yesterday, On Bended Knee (which they sang onstage with Justin in 2010).

BEYONCÉ
A global superstar who gives every performance her all, Justin says she leaves him in awe.

DID YOU KNOW?
Many artists have influenced Justin, but the first song he ever performed publicly was Matchbox 20's "3 A.M."

ALL ABOARD THE TOUR BUS
PLAY JUSTIN'S BRILLIANT TOUR GAME

How to play:
Place a counter for each player on START, grab a dice and get going.
Take turns to roll the dice and move the number of spaces shown, then follow the instructions on the board.

START

1 The tour sells out in record time. **Jump forward 3 spaces.**

2

3 You accidentally eat JB's rider. **Move back 1 space.**

4

5 Fans mob the tour bus. **Roll again.**

10 Usher drops by to say hi. **Jump forward 3 spaces.**

9

8 Uh–oh. JB's losing his voice. **Head to the time-out zone.**

7 TIME OUT ZONE Roll a 6 to get out.

6

11

12 The bus breaks down. **Roll again.**

13

14 JB's bodyguard squashes you while holding back screaming fans. **Go back 1 space.**

15

16

17 Everyone wants your autograph. **Jump forward 1 space.**

22 You manage to prank Justin. **Move forward 3 spaces.**

21

20

19 Oh no. The bus has left Justin behind at a service station. **Miss a turn.**

18

23

24 Justin's having a bad hair day. **Roll again.**

25

YOU WIN!

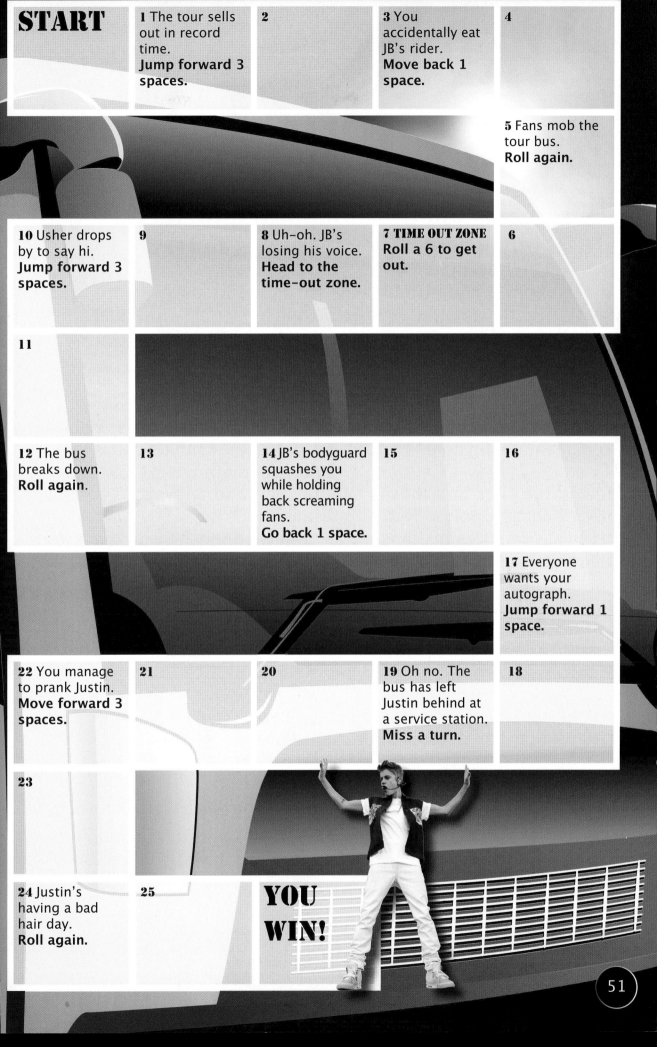

51

FAN-TASTIC

He may be a multi-platinum selling recording artist, but Justin really loves his fans.

Justin is truly grateful to his fans, he knows he owes them everything. "My dreams used to be one-in-a-million chance," he says. "I never forget that none of this would have happened without my fans."

Justin's worldwide army of devoted Biebettes are some of the most important people in his life. Every one of his fans is special to him and Justin loves performing so he can connect with them. "One of my favourite moments in every show is when I get to walk downstage, look into those beautiful eyes and tell you, "If you need me, I'll come running from a thousand miles away." he says. Justin always gives his fans his all, and we know he won't stop for a long time to come.

JUSTIN'S FANS.
Justin's fans come from every walk of life and from every single country all over the world. So it's no wonder that this special group of fans is known by special Bieber names.

THE BELIEBERS: always believe in their hero (and he believes in them).
THE BIEBER ARMY: stands millions strong
THE BIEBERPHILES: they live up to their name totally loving everything JB.
BIEBER BABES AND BIEB BOYS: they are a powerful force indeed.

DID YOU KNOW?
Justin loves seeing his fans holding their hands in the shapes of hearts at his concerts.

JUSTIN GIVES BACK

The most charitable boy in pop...

Justin is fast becoming known for the good things he is doing in this world as much as he is for making music. Many celebrities do charity work, but Justin really stands out. Even when he has a full schedule, he somehow still finds the time to do charity work. His charitable spirit has caused a whole generation of Beliebers to think about giving. Justin truly believes that with his celebrity status he can really make a difference in the world and is determined to do just that.

JUSTIN: WE SALUTE YOU.

Here are just a few examples of the generous star giving back:

Justin has given money, effort and his time to many charitable causes including his Believe Charity Drive and the Make-a-Wish Foundation.

He donates a percentage of money from each concert ticket he sells to his favourite charity – Pencils of Promise. (A group founded and run by his manager Scooter Braun's brother.) The amount of money he raised for Pencils of Promise has built at least 25 schools.

He has also given a great deal of his time towards anti-bullying.

On his 18th birthday, he asked his fans to mark his milestone birthday by giving to those in need.

He makes secret visits to Children's Hospitals around the world including London's Great Ormond Street Hospital for Children and spent time with young patients, many of whom were seriously ill.

THE ULTIMATE JUSTIN BIEBER QUIZ

THINK YOU'VE GOT A BAD CASE OF BIEBER FEVER?

TAKE OUR ULTIMATE JB TRIVIA CHALLENGE AND FIND OUT IF YOU'RE HIS NUMBER ONE FAN.

1 WHAT IS JUSTIN'S MIDDLE NAME?

2 WHAT YEAR WAS JUSTIN BORN?

3 WHAT PROVINCE OF CANADA WAS JUSTIN BORN IN?

4 WHAT WAS JUSTIN'S FIRST SINGLE?

5 WHAT WAS JUSTIN'S FIRST ALBUM CALLED?

6 BESIDES ENGLISH, WHAT LANGUAGE IS JUSTIN FLUENT IN?

7 HOW MANY INSTRUMENTS CAN JUSTIN PLAY?

8 WHICH OF THESE STARS SHARES JB'S BIRTHDAY? SELENA GOMEZ, LADY GAGA OR KE$HA

9 WHAT IS JUSTIN'S FAVOURITE FOOD?

10 HOW OLD WAS JUSTIN WHEN HE HAD HIS FIRST KISS?

11 WHICH SINGER ALSO WANTED TO MENTOR JUSTIN, ALTHOUGH USHER ULTIMATELY WON OUT?

12 WHAT ACTION STAR IS JB TOTALLY OBSESSED WITH?

Answers on Page 61!

THE FUTURE

There's no doubt that this has been an amazing year for this pop icon but knowing Justin we haven't seen anything yet. So what's next?

Justin's worked so hard for his success, but the star knows he can't afford to relax if his success is to continue. Once you reach the top the pressure is there to stay at the top. Justin knows he has to keep on growing as an artist and doing new things to keep himself and his fans around the world happy. He's always looking for ways to keep pushing boundaries forwards. Something he's been working on with his latest album and his sell-out world arena tour, wowing his fans with some very special effects.

"I want to keep growing as an artist, as an entertainer and basically perfect my craft," he says. "I want to be the best I can be."

Justin has become a part of our everyday world - a sign of true fame. He's become a pop icon and a role model to millions of fans around the world. And we can't wait to see what he achieves next on his amazing journey. One thing's for sure, he'll be sharing it with the people who are the most important to him - his fans.

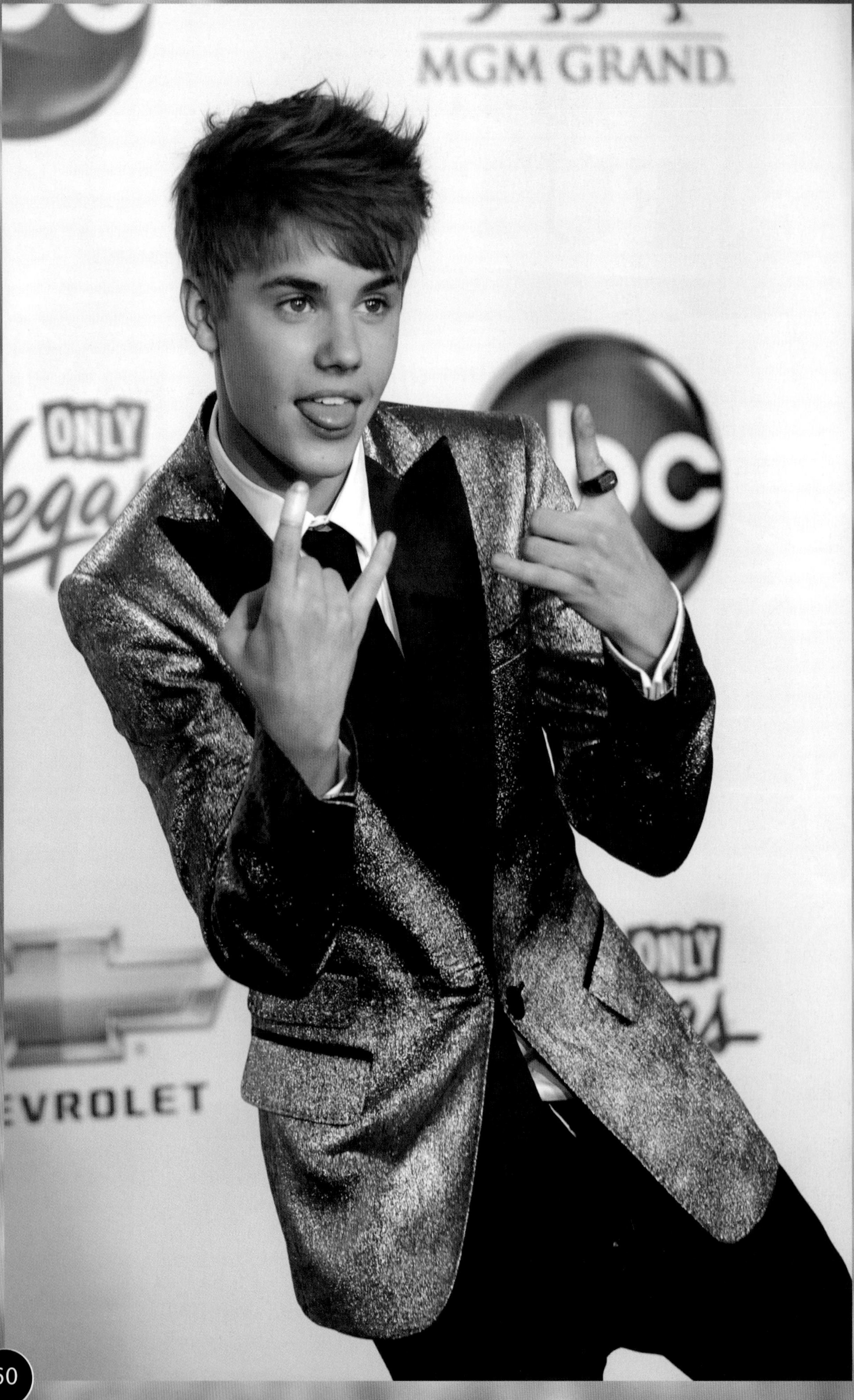
MGM GRAND
ONLY
EVROLET
ONLY

ANSWERS

How did you do?

THE BIG CROSSWORD

FACT OR FICTION?
1   True
2   True
3   False
4   True
5   False
6   True
7   False
8   False

SCRAMBLED LYRICS
1   Believe
2   Baby
3   Boyfriend
4   Pray
5   Eenie, meenie, miney, mo

THE ULTIMATE JUSTIN BIEBER QUIZ
1   Drew
2   1994
3   Ontario
4   One Time
5   My World
6   French
7   4
8   Ke$ha
9   Spaghetti bolognaise
10 13
11 Justin Timberlake
12 Chuck Norris

SPOT THE DIFFERENCE

WHERE'S JUSTIN?